双语名著无障碍阅读丛书

经典集锦

飞鸟集

Stray Birds

［印度］泰戈尔 著

郑振铎 译

中国出版集团

中译出版社

图书在版编目(CIP)数据

飞鸟集:英汉对照 /(英)泰戈尔著;郑振铎译 . —北京:中译出版社,
2017.6
    (双语名著无障碍阅读丛书)
    ISBN 978-7-5001-5273-6

    Ⅰ.①飞…   Ⅱ.①泰… ②郑…   Ⅲ.①英语-汉语-对照读物 ②诗
集-印度-现代   Ⅳ.①H319.4∶I

    中国版本图书馆CIP数据核字(2017)第108697号

出版发行 / 中译出版社
地　　址 / 北京市西城区车公庄大街甲4号物华大厦6层
电　　话 / (010) 68359827; 　68359303(发行部); 　53601537(编辑部)
邮　　编 / 100044
传　　真 / (010) 68357870
电子邮箱 / book@ctph.com.cn
网　　址 / http://www.ctph.com.cn

总 策 划 / 张高里
策划编辑 / 胡晓凯
责任编辑 / 胡晓凯　范祥镇

封面设计 / 潘　峰
排　　版 / 北京竹页文化传媒有限公司

经　　销 / 新华书店

规　　格 / 710毫米×1000毫米　1/16
印　　张 / 7.25
字　　数 / 110千字
版　　次 / 2017年6月第一版
印　　次 / 2017年6月第一次

ISBN 978-7-5001-5273-6　　定价:16.00元

多年以来，中译出版社有限公司（原中国对外翻译出版有限公司）凭借国内一流的翻译和出版实力及资源，精心策划、出版了大批双语读物，在海内外读者中和业界内产生了良好、深远的影响，形成了自己鲜明的出版特色。

二十世纪八九十年代出版的英汉（汉英）对照"一百丛书"，声名远扬，成为一套最权威、最有特色且又实用的双语读物，影响了一代又一代英语学习者和中华传统文化研究者、爱好者；还有"英若诚名剧译丛""中华传统文化精粹丛书""美丽英文书系"，这些优秀的双语读物，有的畅销，有的常销不衰反复再版，有的被选为大学英语阅读教材，受到广大读者的喜爱，获得了良好的社会效益和经济效益。

"双语名著无障碍阅读丛书"是中译专门为中学生和英语学习者精心打造的又一品牌，是一个新的双语读物系列，具有以下特点：

选题创新——该系列图书是国内第一套为中小学生量身打造的双语名著读物，所选篇目均为教育部颁布的语文新课标必读书目，或为中学生以及同等文化水平的

　　社会读者喜闻乐见的世界名著，重新编译为英汉（汉英）对照的双语读本。这些书既给青少年读者提供了成长过程中不可或缺的精神食粮，又让他们领略到原著的精髓和魅力，对他们更好地学习英文大有裨益；同时，丛书中入选的《论语》《茶馆》《家》等汉英对照读物，亦是热爱中国传统文化的中外读者所共知的经典名篇，能使读者充分享受阅读经典的无限乐趣。

　　无障碍阅读——中学生阅读世界文学名著的原著会遇到很多生词和文化难点。针对这一情况，我们给每一本读物原文中的较难词汇和不易理解之处都加上了注释，在内文的版式设计上也采取英汉（或汉英）对照方式，扫清了学生阅读时的障碍。

　　优良品质——中译双语读物多年来在读者中享有良好口碑，这得益于作者和出版者对于图书质量的不懈追求。"双语名著无障碍阅读丛书"继承了中译双语读物的优良传统——精选的篇目、优秀的译文、方便实用的注解，秉承着对每一个读者负责的精神，竭力打造精品图书。

　　愿这套丛书成为广大读者的良师益友，愿读者在英语学习和传统文化学习两方面都取得新的突破。

Rabindranath Tagore

1

Stray birds of summer come to my window to sing and fly away. And yellow leaves of autumn, which have no songs, **flutter**[①] and fall there with a sign.

2

O **Troupe**[②] of little **vagrants**[③] of the world, leave your footprints in my words.

3

The world puts off its mask of vastness to its lover. It becomes small as one song, as one kiss of the **eternal**[④].

4

It is the tears of the earth that keep her smiles in bloom.

5

The mighty desert is burning for the love of a blade of grass who shakes her head and laughs and flies away.

1

夏天的飞鸟，飞到我窗前唱歌，又飞去了。

秋天的黄叶，它们没有什么可唱，只叹息一声，飞落在那里。

2

世界上的一队小小的漂泊者呀，请留下你们的足印在我的文字里。

3

世界对着它的爱人，把它浩瀚的面具揭下了。

它变小了，小如一首歌，小如一回永恒的接吻。

4

是"地"的泪点，使她的微笑保持着青春不谢。

5

广漠无垠的沙漠热烈地追求着一叶绿草的爱，但她摇摇头，笑起来，飞了开去。

---

① flutter ['flʌtə] v. 飘动，摆动

② troupe [tru:p] n. 群，队

③ vagrant ['veigrənt] n. 流浪者

④ eternal [i'tə:nəl] a. 永久的，不朽的

6

If you **shed**[1] tears when you miss the sun, you also miss the stars.

7

The sands in your way beg for your song and your movement, dancing water. Will you carry the burden of their **lameness**[2]?

8

Her wishful face **haunts**[3] my dreams like the rain at night.

9

Once we dreamt that we were strangers. We wake up to find that we were dear to each other.

10

Sorrow is **hushed**[4] into peace in my heart like the evening among the silent trees.

11

Some unseen fingers, like an **idle**[5] breeze, are playing upon my heart the music of the ripples.

6

如果错过了太阳时你流了泪，那么你也要错过群星了。

7

跳舞着的流水呀，在你途中的泥沙，要求你的歌声，你的流动呢。你肯挟跛足的泥沙而俱下么？

8

她的热切的脸，如夜雨似的，搅扰着我的梦魂。

9

有一次，我们梦见大家都是不相识的。
我们醒了，却知道我们原是相亲相爱的。

10

忧思在我的心里平静下去，正如黄昏在寂静的林中。

11

有些看不见的手指，如懒懒的微飔似的，正在我的心上，奏着潺湲的乐声。

① shed [ʃed] v. 使流出，使涌出

② lameness [leimnis] n. 跛，残废

③ haunt [hɔ:nt] v.（思想、回忆等）萦绕在……，使苦恼

④ hush [hʌʃ] v. 使安静，使平静

⑤ idle ['aidl] a. 闲散的，懒惰的

12

"What language is **thine**[1], O sea? "
"The language of eternal question."
"What language is **thy**[2] answer, O sky?"
"The language of eternal silence."

13

Listen, my heart, to the whispers of the world with which it makes love to you.

14

The mystery of creation is like the darkness of night—it is great. **Delusions**[3] of knowledge are like the fog of the morning.

15

Do not seat your love upon a **precipice**[4] because it is high.

16

I sit at my window this morning where the world like a **passer-by**[5] stops for a moment, nods to me and goes.

17

These little thoughts are the **rustle**[6] of leaves; they have their whisper of joy in my mind.

12

"海水呀，你说的是什么？"

"是永恒的疑问。"

"天空呀，你回答的话是什么？"

"是永恒的沉默。"

13

静静地听，我的心呀，听那"世界"的低语，这是他对你的爱的表示呀。

14

创造的神秘，有如夜间的黑暗，——是伟大的。而知识的幻影，不过如晨间之雾。

15

不要因为峭壁是高的，便让你的爱情坐在峭壁上。

16

我今晨坐在窗前，"世界"如一个过路人似的，停留了一会，向我点点头又走过去了。

17

这些微思，是树叶的簌簌之声呀；他们在我的心里，愉悦地微语着。

① thine [θain] *n.* [thou 的物主代词绝对形式] 你的东西

② thy [ðai] *a.* 你的

③ delusion [di'lu:ʒən] *n.* 妄想，错觉

④ precipice ['presipis] *n.* 悬崖，峭壁

⑤ passer-by ['pɑ:səbai] *n.* 过路人

⑥ rustle ['rʌsl] *n.* 沙沙声，窸窣声

18

What you are you do not see, what you see is your shadow.

19

My wishes are fools, they shout across thy song, my Master. Let me but listen.

20

I cannot choose the best. The best chooses me.

21

They throw their shadows before them who carry their **lantern**[①] on their back.

22

That I exist is a **perpetual**[②] surprise which is life.

23

"We, the rustling leaves, have a voice that answers the storms, but who are you so silent?"

"I am a **mere**[③] flower."

18

你看不见你的真相，你所看见的，只是你的影子。

19

主呀，我的那些愿望真是愚傻呀，它们杂在你的歌声中喧叫着呢。让我只是静听着吧。

20

我不能选择那最好的。是那最好的选择我。

21

那些把灯背在他们的背上的人，把他们的影子投到他们前面去。

22

我的存在，乃是所谓生命的一个永久的奇迹。

23

"我们，萧萧的树叶，都有声响回答那暴风雨，你是谁呢，那样地沉默着？"
"我不过是一朵花。"

① lantern ['læntən] *n.* 灯笼，提灯

② perpetual [pə'petʃuəl] *a.* 永远的，永恒的

③ mere [miə] *a.* 仅仅的，只不过

24

Rest belongs to the work as the eyelids to the eyes.

25

Man is a born child, his power is the power of growth.

26

God expects answers for the flowers he sends us, not for the sun and the earth.

27

The light that plays, like a **naked**[①] child, among the green leaves happily knows not that man can lie.

28

O Beauty, find thyself in love, not in the **flattery**[②] of thy **mirror**[③].

29

My heart beats her waves at the shore of the world and writes upon it her **signature**[④] in tears with the words, "I love thee."

24

休息之隶属于工作，正如眼睑之隶属于眼睛。

25

人是一个初生的孩子，他的力量，就是生长的力量。

26

上帝希望我们酬答他的，在于他送给我们的花朵，而不在于太阳和土地。

27

光如一个裸体的孩子，快快活活地在绿叶当中游戏，他不知道人是会欺诈的。

28

啊，美呀，在爱中找你自己吧，不要到你镜子的谄谀中去找呀。

29

我的心中激着她的波浪在"世界"的海岸上，蘸着眼泪在上边写着她的题记："我爱你。"

① naked ['neikid] *a.* 赤身裸体的

② flattery ['flætəri] *n.* 恭维，讨好

③ mirror ['mirə] *n.* 镜子

④ signature ['signətʃə] *n.* 签字，签名

30

"Moon, for what do you wait?"
"To **salute**[1] the sun for whom I must **make way**[2]."

31

The trees come up to my window like the **yearning**[3] voice of the dumb earth.

32

His own mornings are new surprises to God.

33

Life finds its wealth by the **claims**[4] of the world, and its worth by the claims of love.

34

The dry river-bed finds no thanks for its past.

35

The bird wishes it were a cloud. The cloud wishes it were a bird.

30

"月儿呀，你在等候什么呢？"
"要致敬意于我必须给他让路的太阳。"

31

绿树长到了我的窗前，仿佛是喑哑的大地发出的渴望的声音。

32

上帝自己的清晨，在他自己看来也是新奇的。

33

生命因了"世界"的要求，得到他的资产，因了爱的要求，得到他的价值。

34

干的河床，并不感谢他的过去。

35

鸟儿愿为一朵云。
云儿愿为一只鸟。

① salute [sɑ:'lu:t] *v.* 向……致意，向……打招呼

② make way 让路

③ yearning [jə:niŋ] *a.* 渴望的，向往的

④ claim [kleim] *n.* 得到某事物的要求

36

The **waterfall**[1] sings, "I find my song, when I find my freedom."

37

I cannot tell why this heart **languishes**[2] in silence. It is for small needs it never asks, or knows or remembers.

38

Woman, when you move about in your household service your limbs sing like a hill stream among its **pebbles**[3].

39

The sun goes to cross the Western sea, leaving its last **salutation**[4] to the East.

40

Do not blame your food because you have no **appetite**[5].

41

The trees, like the longings of the earth, stand a-tiptoe to **peep**[6] at the heaven.

36

瀑布歌道："我得到自由时便有了歌声了。"

① waterfall ['wɔ:təfɔ:l] *n.* 瀑布

37

我不能说出这心为什么那样默默地颓丧着。

那小小的需要，他是永不要求，永不知道，永不记着的。

② languish ['læŋgwiʃ] *v.* 失去活力，变得衰弱无力

38

妇人，你在料理家事的时候，你的手足歌唱着，正如山间的溪水歌唱着在小石中流过。

③ pebble ['pebl] *n.* 卵石，石子

39

太阳横过西方的海面时，对着东方，致他的最后的敬礼。

④ salutation [ˌsælju:'teiʃən] *n.* 招呼，致意

40

不要因为你自己没有胃口，而去责备你的食物。

⑤ appetite ['æpitait] *n.* 食欲，胃口

41

群树如表示大地的愿望似的，竖趾立着，向天空窥望。

⑥ peep [pi:p] *v.* 偷看，窥探

42

You smiled and talked to me of nothing and I felt that for this I had been waiting long.

43

The fish in the water is silent, the animal on the earth is noisy, the bird in the air is singing. But Man has in him the silence of the sea, the noise of the earth and the music of the air.

44

The world rushes on over the **strings**① of the **lingering**② heart making the music of sadness.

45

He has made his weapons his gods. When his weapons win he is defeated himself.

46

God finds himself by creating.

47

Shadow, with her **veil**③ drawn, follows Light in secret **meekness**④, with her silent steps of love.

42

你微微地笑着，不同我说什么话，而我觉得，为了这个，我已等待得久了。

43

水里的游鱼是沉默的，陆地上的兽类是喧闹的，空中的飞鸟是歌唱着的；但是人类却兼有了海里的沉默，地上的喧闹，与空中的音乐。

44

"世界"在踌躇之心的琴弦上跑过去，奏出忧郁的乐声。

① string [striŋ] *n.*（乐器的）弦

② lingering ['liŋgəriŋ] *a.* 拖延的，逗留的，留恋的

45

他把他的刀剑当作他的上帝。
当他的刀剑胜利时他自己却失败了。

46

上帝从创造中找到他自己。

47

阴影戴上她的面幕，秘密地，温顺地，用她的沉默的爱的脚步，跟在"光"后边。

③ veil [veil] *n.* 面纱

④ meekness [mi: knis] *n.* 温顺，谦恭

48

The stars are not afraid to appear like **fireflies**①.

49

I thank thee that I am none of the wheels of power but I am one with the living creatures that are crushed by it.

50

The mind, sharp but not broad, sticks at every point but does not move.

51

Your **idol**② is **shattered**③ in the dust to prove that God's dust is greater than your idol.

52

Man does not reveal himself in his history, he struggles up through it.

53

While the glass lamp **rebukes**④ the **earthen**⑤ for calling it cousin the moon rises, and the glass lamp, with a **bland**⑥ smile, calls her, "My dear, dear sister."

48

群星不怕显得像萤火虫那样。

49

谢谢上帝，我不是一个权力的轮子，而是被压在这轮下的活人之一。

50

心是尖锐的，不是宽博的，它执着在每一点上，却并不活动。

51

你的偶像委散在尘土中了，这可证明上帝的尘土比你的偶像还伟大。

52

人在他的历史中表现不出他自己，他在历史中奋斗着露出头角。

53

玻璃灯因为瓦灯叫他做表兄而责备瓦灯，但当明月出来时，玻璃灯却温和地微笑着，叫明月为——"我亲爱的，亲爱的姊姊。"

① firefly ['faiəflai] *n.*【昆虫】萤火虫

② idol ['aidəl] *n.* 偶像

③ shatter ['ʃætə] *v.* 把……打碎，使粉碎

④ rebuke [ri'bju:k] *v.* 指责，训斥

⑤ earthen ['ə:θən] *a.* 泥制的

⑥ bland [blænd] *a.* 温和的，和蔼的，文雅的

54

Like the meeting of the **seagulls**[1] and the waves we meet and come near. The seagulls fly off, the waves roll away and we depart.

55

My day is done, and I am like a boat drawn on the beach, listening to the dance-music of the tide in the evening.

56

Life is given to us, we earn it by giving it.

57

We come nearest to the great when we are great in **humility**[2].

58

The **sparrow**[3] is sorry for the **peacock**[4] at the burden of its tail.

59

Never be afraid of the moments—thus sings the voice of the **everlasting**[5].

54

我们如海鸥之与波涛相遇似的，遇见了，走近了。海鸥飞去，波涛滚滚的流开，我们也分别了。

55

日间的工作完了，于是我像一只拖在海滩上的小船，静静地听着晚潮跳舞的乐声。

56

我们的生命是天赋的，我们唯有献出生命，才能得到生命。

57

当我们是大为谦卑的时候，便是我们最近于伟大的时候。

58

麻雀看见孔雀负担着它的翎尾，替它担忧。

59

决不要害怕刹那——永恒之声这样地唱着。

① seagull ['si:,gʌl] *n.* 海鸥

② humility [hju:'miləti] *n.* 谦逊，谦恭

③ sparrow ['spærəu] *n.* 家麻雀，家雀

④ peacock ['pi:kɔk] *n.* 孔雀

⑤ everlasting [,evə'lɑ:stiŋ] *a.* 永恒的，永久的

60

The **hurricane**① seeks the shortest road by the no-road, and suddenly ends its search in the Nowhere.

61

Take my wine in my own cup, friend. It loses its **wreath**② of **foam**③ when poured into that of others.

62

The perfect decks itself in beauty for the love of the Imperfect.

63

God says to man, "I heal you therefore I hurt, love you therefore punish."

64

Thank the flame for its light, but do not forget the lampholder standing in the shade with **constancy**④ of patience.

65

Tiny grass, your steps are small, but you **possess**⑤ the earth under your **tread**⑥.

60

飓风于无路之中寻求最短之路，又突然地在"无何有之国"终止它的寻求了。

61

在我自己的杯中，饮了我的酒吧，朋友。

一倒在别人的杯里，这酒的腾跳的泡沫便要消失了。

62

"完全"为了对"不全"的爱，把自己装饰得美丽。

63

上帝对人说道："我医治你，所以要伤害你，我爱你，所以要惩罚你。"

64

谢谢火焰给你光明，但是不要忘了那执灯的人，他是坚忍地站在黑暗当中呢。

65

小草呀，你的足步虽小，但是你拥有你足下的土地。

---

① hurricane ['hʌrikən] *n.* 飓风，风暴

② wreath [ri:θ] *n.* 圈状物，环状物

③ foam [fəum] *n.* 泡沫

④ constancy ['kɔnst(ə)nsi] *n.* 坚定不移，坚贞，坚决

⑤ possess [pə'zes] *v.* 拥有

⑥ tread [tred] *n.* 踩，踏

66

The **infant**[1] flower opens its bud and cries, "Dear World, please do not **fade**[2]."

67

God grows **weary**[3] of great kingdoms, but never of little flowers.

68

Wrong cannot afford defeat but Right can.

69

"I give my whole water in joy," sings the waterfall, "though little of it is enough for the thirsty."

70

Where is the fountain that throws up these flowers in a **ceaseless**[4] **outbreak**[5] of **ecstasy**[6]?

71

The woodcutter's axe begged for its handle from the tree. The tree gave it.

① infant ['inf(ə)nt] *n.* 婴儿，幼儿

② fade [feid] *v.* 消逝，变暗淡，凋落

③ weary ['wiəri] *a.* 疲倦的，厌烦的

④ ceaseless ['si:slis] *a.* 不停的，不断，无休止的

⑤ outbreak ['autbreik] *n.* 爆发，突然发生

⑥ ecstasy ['ekstəsi] *n.* 狂喜

66

幼花开放了它的蓓蕾，叫道："亲爱的世界呀，请不要萎谢了。"

67

上帝对于大帝国会生厌，却决不会厌恶那小小的花朵。

68

错误经不起失败，但是真理却不怕失败。

69

瀑布歌道："虽然渴者只要少许的水便够了，我却很快活地给予了我全部的水。

70

把那些花朵抛掷上去的那一阵子无休无止的狂欢大喜的劲儿，其源泉是在哪里呢？

71

樵夫的斧头，问树要斧柄。
树便给了他。

72

In my **solitude**① of heart I feel the sigh of this **widowed**② evening veiled with mist and rain.

73

Chastity③ is a wealth that comes from **abundance**④ of love.

74

The mist, like love, plays upon the heart of the hills and brings out surprises of beauty.

75

We read the world wrong and say that it **deceives**⑤ us.

76

The poet wind is out over the sea and the forest to seek his own voice.

77

Every child comes with the message that God is not yet **discouraged**⑥ of man.

72

这寂独的黄昏，幕着雾与雨，我在我的心的孤寂里，感觉到它的叹息了。

73

贞操是从丰富的爱情中生出来的资产。

74

雾，像爱情一样，在山峰的心上游戏，生出种种美丽的变幻。

75

我们把世界看错了，反说他欺骗我们。

76

诗人的风，正出经海洋和森林，求它自己的歌声。

77

每一个孩子生出时所带的神示说：上帝对于人尚未灰心失望呢。

① solitude ['sɔlitju:d] *n.* 孤独
② widowed ['widəud] *a.* 丧偶的
③ chastity ['tʃæstiti] *n.* 贞节，节操
④ abundance [ə'bʌnd(ə)ns] *n.* 充足，大量，丰富
⑤ deceive [di'si:v] *v.* 欺骗
⑥ discouraged [di'skʌridʒd] *a.* 灰心的，泄气的，沮丧的

78

The grass seeks her crowd in the earth. The tree seeks his solitude of the sky.

79

Man **barricades**[①] against himself.

80

Your voice, my friend, wanders in my heart, like the **muffled**[②] sound of the sea among these listening pines.

81

What is this unseen flame of darkness whose sparks are the stars?

82

Let life be beautiful like summer flowers and death like autumn leaves.

83

He who wants to do good knocks at the gate; he who loves finds the gate open.

78

绿草求她地上的伴侣。
树木求他天空的寂寞。

79

人对他自己建筑起堤防来。

80

我的朋友，你的语声飘荡在我的心里，像那海水的低吟之声，绕缭在静听着的松林之间。

81

这个不可见的黑暗之火焰，以繁星为其火花的，到底是什么呢？

82

使生如夏花之绚烂，死如秋叶之静美。

83

那想做好人的，在门外敲着门，那爱人的，看见门敞开着。

① barricade [ˌbæri'keid] v. 设街垒（或路障）于，用街垒阻塞；阻塞，堵塞

② muffled ['mʌfld] a. 听不清的

84

In death the many becomes one; in life the one becomes many. Religion will be one when God is dead.

85

The artist is the lover of Nature, therefore he is her slave and her master.

86

"How far are you from me, O Fruit?"
"I am hidden in your heart, O Flower."

87

This longing is for the one who is felt in the dark, but not seen in the day.

88

"You are the big drop of **dew**[1] under the **lotus**[2] leaf, I am the smaller one on its upper side," said the dew drop to the lake.

89

The **scabbard**[3] is **content**[4] to be dull when it protects the **keenness**[5] of the sword.

84

在死的时候，众多合而为一，在生的时候，这"一"化而为众多。

上帝死了的时候，宗教便将合而为一。

85

艺术家是自然的情人，所以他是自然的奴隶，也是自然的主人。

86

"你离我有多少远呢，果实呀？"

"我是藏在你的心里呢，花呀。"

87

这个渴望是为了那个在黑夜里感觉得到、在大白天里却看不见的人。

① dew ['dju:] *n.* 露水，露

② lotus ['ləutəs] *n.* 莲花

③ scabbard ['skæbəd] *n.* （刀、剑等的）鞘

④ content [kən'tent] *a.* 满意的，满足的

⑤ keenness ['ki:nnəs] *n.* 敏锐，锐利

88

露珠对湖水说道："你，是在荷叶下面的大露珠，我是在荷叶上面的较小的露珠。"

89

刀鞘保护刀的锋利，它自己则满足于它的迟钝。

90

In darkness the One appears as **uniform**①; in the light the One appears as **manifold**②.

91

The great earth makes herself **hospitable**③ with the help of the grass.

92

The birth and death of the leaves are the rapid **whirls**④ of the **eddy**⑤ whose wider circles move slowly among stars.

93

Power said to the world, "You are mine."
The world kept it prisoner on her throne.
Love said to the world, "I am thine."
The world gave it the freedom of her house.

94

The mist is like the earth's desire. It hides the sun for whom she cries.

95

Be still, my heart, these great trees are **prayers**⑥.

90

在黑暗中"一"视若一体，在光亮中，"一"便视若众多。

91

大地借助于绿草，显出她自己的殷勤好客。

92

绿叶的生与死乃是旋风的急骤的旋转，它的更广大的旋转的圈子乃是在天上繁星之间徐缓的转动。

93

权势对世界说道："你是我的。"
世界便把威权囚禁在她的宝座下面。
爱情对世界说道："我是你的。"
世界便给予爱情以在她屋内来往的自由。

94

浓雾仿佛是大地的愿望。
它藏起了太阳，而太阳乃是她所呼求的。

95

安静些吧，我的心，这些大树都是祈祷者呀。

---

① uniform ['ju:nifɔ:m] *a.* 统一的，一致的

② manifold ['mænifəuld] *a.* 多样的，繁多的

③ hospitable [hɔ'spitəb(ə)l] *a.* 款待周到的，殷勤的，好客的

④ whirl [wɜ:l] *n.* 回旋，旋转

⑤ eddy ['edi] *n.* 涡流，漩涡

⑥ prayer [preiə] *n.* 祈祷人，祷告者

96

The noise of the moment **scoffs**[1] at the music of the Eternal.

97

I think of other ages that floated upon the stream of life and love and death and are forgotten, and I feel the freedom of **passing away**[2].

98

The sadness of my soul is her bride's veil. It waits to be lifted in the night.

99

Death's stamp gives value to the coin of life; making it possible to buy with life what is truly precious.

100

The cloud stood **humbly**[3] in a corner of the sky. The morning crowned it with **splendour**[4].

101

The dust receives **insult**[5] and in return offers her flowers.

96

瞬刻的喧声，讥笑着永恒的音乐。

97

我想起了浮泛在生与爱与死的川流上的许多别的时代，以及这些时代之被遗忘，我便感觉到离开尘世的自由了。

98

我灵魂里的忧郁就是她的新妇的面纱。
这面纱等候着在夜间卸去。

99

死之印记给生的钱币以价值；使它能够用生命来购买那真正的宝物。

100

白云谦逊地站在天之一隅。
晨光给他戴上了霞彩。

101

尘土受到损辱，却以她的花朵来报答。

① scoff [skɔf] v. 嘲笑，愚弄

② pass away 去世，死

③ humbly ['hʌmbli] ad. 谦逊地，谦恭地

④ splendour ['splendə] n. 光彩，光辉

⑤ insult ['insʌlt] n. 侮辱，无礼，冒犯

102

Do not **linger**① to gather flowers to keep them, but walk on, for flowers will keep themselves blooming all your way.

103

Roots are the branches down in the earth. Branches are roots in the air.

104

The music of the far-away summer flutters around the autumn seeking its **former**② nest.

105

Do not **insult**③ your friend by lending him **merits**④ from your own pocket.

106

The touch of the nameless days **clings**⑤ to my heart like **mosses**⑥ round the old tree.

107

The echo **mocks**⑦ her origin to prove she is the original.

102

只管走过去，不必逗留着采了花朵来保存，因为一路上，花朵自会继续开放的。

103

根是地下的枝。
枝是空中的根。

104

远远去了的夏之音乐，翱翔于秋间，寻求它的旧垒。

105

不要从你自己的袋里掏出勋绩借给你的朋友，这是污辱他的。

106

无名的日子的感触，攀缘在我的心上，正像那绿色的苔藓，攀缘在老树的周身。

107

回声嘲笑着她的原声，以证明她是原声。

① linger ['liŋgə] v. 徘徊，继续逗留，留恋

② former ['fɔ:mə] a. 先前的，以前的，从前的

③ insult [in'sʌlt] v. 侮辱，辱骂

④ merit ['merit] n. 功绩

⑤ cling [kliŋ] v. 缠住，抱住，萦绕

⑥ moss [mɔs] n. 苔藓

⑦ mock [mɔk] v. 嘲弄，模仿

108

God is **ashamed**[1] when the **prosperous**[2] **boasts**[3] of his special favour.

109

I cast my own shadow upon my path, because I have a lamp that has not been lighted.

110

Man goes into the noisy crowd to drown his own **clamour**[4] of silence.

111

That which ends in **exhaustion**[5] is death, but the perfect ending is in the endless.

112

The sun has his simple robe of light. The clouds are **decked**[6] with **gorgeousness**[7].

113

The hills are like shouts of children who raise their arms, trying to catch stars.

108

当富贵利达的人夸说他得到上帝的特别恩惠时，上帝却羞了。

109

我投射我自己的影子在我的路上，因为我有一盏还没有燃点起来的明灯。

110

人走进喧哗的群众里去，为的是要淹没他自己的沉默的呼号。

111

终止于衰竭的是"死亡"，但"圆满"却终止于无穷。

112

太阳只穿一件朴素的光衣。白云却披了灿烂的裙裾。

113

山峰如群儿之喧嚷，举起他们的双臂，想去捉天上的星星。

① ashamed [ə'ʃeimd] *a.* 羞耻的，羞愧的，惭愧的
② prosperous ['prɒsp(ə)rəs] *a.* 成功的，富裕的
③ boast [bəust] *v.* 自夸，夸耀
④ clamour ['klæmə] *n.* 吵闹，吵嚷
⑤ exhaustion [ig'zɔ:stʃ(ə)n] *n.* 疲惫不堪，极度疲劳，筋疲力尽
⑥ deck [dek] *v.* 装饰，点缀
⑦ gorgeousness ['gɔ:dʒəsnis] *n.* 绚丽，华丽，豪华

114

The road is lonely in its crowd for it is not loved.

115

The power that boasts of its **mischiefs**[1] is laughed at by the yellow leaves that fall, and clouds that pass by.

116

The earth **hums**[2] to me today in the sun, like a woman at her **spinning**[3], some **ballad**[4] of the ancient time in a forgotten tongue.

117

The grass-blade is worthy of the great world where it grows.

118

Dream is a wife who must talk. Sleep is a husband who silently suffers.

119

The night kisses the fading day whispering to his ear, "I am death, your mother. I am to give you fresh birth."

114

道路虽然拥挤，却是寂寞的，因为它是不被爱的。

115

权势以它的恶行自夸；落下的黄叶与浮游过的云片却在笑它。

116

今天大地在太阳光里向我营营哼鸣，像一个织着布的妇人，用一种已经被忘却的语言，哼着一些古代的歌曲。

117

绿草是无愧于它所生长的伟大世界的。

118

梦是一个一定要谈话的妻子。
睡眠是一个默默地忍受的丈夫。

119

夜与逝去的日子接吻，轻轻地在他耳旁说道："我是死，是你的母亲。我就要给你以新的生命。"

① mischief ['mistʃif] *n.* 损害，伤害，危害，祸害

② hum [hʌm] *v.* 哼，哼曲子

③ spinning ['spiniŋ] *n.* 纺织

④ ballad ['bæləd] *n.* 民谣，民歌，歌谣

120

I feel thy beauty, dark night, like that of the loved woman when she has put out the lamp.

121

I carry in my world that **flourishes**[1] the worlds that have failed.

122

Dear friend, I feel the silence of your great thoughts of many a **deepening**[2] **eventide**[3] on this beach when I listen to these waves.

123

The bird thinks it is an act of kindness to give the fish a life in the air.

124

"In the moon thou sendest thy love letters to me," said the night to the sun. "I leave my answers in tears upon the grass."

125

The Great is a born child; when he dies he gives his great childhood to the world.

120

黑夜呀，我感觉得你的美了，你的美如一个可爱的妇人，当她把灯灭了的时候。

121

我把在那些已逝去的世界上的繁荣带到我的世界上来。

122

亲爱的朋友呀，当我静听着海涛时，我有好几次在暮色深沉的黄昏里，在这个海岸上，感到你的伟大思想的沉默了。

123

鸟以为把鱼举在空中是一种慈善的举动。

124

夜对太阳说道："在月亮中，你送了你的情书给我。""我已在绿草上留下我的流着泪点的回答了。"

125

伟人是一个天生的孩子，当他死时，他把他的伟大的孩提时代给了世界。

① flourish ['flauriʃ] v. 繁茂，茂盛，繁荣

② deepen ['di:pəniŋ] v. 加深

③ eventide ['i:v(ə)ntaid] n. 黄昏，傍晚，薄暮

126

Not hammer-strokes, but dance of the water sings the pebbles into perfection.

127

Bees **sip**[1] honey from flowers and hum their thanks when they leave. The **gaudy**[2] butterfly is sure that the flowers owe thanks to him.

128

To be **outspoken**[3] is easy when you do not wait to speak the complete truth.

129

Asks the Possible to the Impossible, "Where is your dwelling-place?"
"In the dreams of the **impotent**[4]," comes the answer.

130

If you shut your door to all errors truth will be shut out.

131

I hear some rustle of things behind my sadness of heart—I cannot see them.

126

不是槌的打击，乃是水的载歌载舞，使鹅卵石臻于完美。

127

蜜蜂从花中啜蜜，离开时营营地道谢。
浮夸的蝴蝶却相信花是应该向他道谢的。

128

如果你不等待着要说出完全的真理，那么把话说出来是很容易的。

129

"可能"问"不可能"道："你住在什么地方呢？"
它回答道："在那无能为力者的梦境里。"

130

如果你把所有的错误都关在门外时，真理也要被关在外面了。

131

我听见有些东西在我心的忧闷后面萧萧作响，——我不能看见它们。

① sip [sip] *v.* 啜，一点一点地喝

② gaudy ['gɔ:di] *a.* 艳丽的，浮华的

③ outspoken [aut'spəuk(ə)n] *a.* 直言的，坦率的

④ impotent ['impət(ə)nt] *a.* 无力的，衰弱的

132

Leisure[1] in its activity is work. The stillness of the sea stirs in waves.

133

The leaf becomes flower when it loves. The flower becomes fruit when it worships[2].

134

The roots below the earth claim no rewards for making the branches fruitful.

135

This rainy evening the wind is restless. I look at the swaying[3] branches and ponder[4] over the greatness of all things.

136

Storm of midnight, like a giant child awakened in the untimely dark, has begun to play and shout.

137

Thou raisest thy waves vainly[5] to follow thy lover, O sea, thou lonely bride of the storm.

① leisure ['leʒə] *n.* 空闲，
　闲暇

② worship ['wə:ʃip] *v.* 崇
　敬，爱慕

③ sway [swei] *v.* 摇动，摆
　动

④ ponder ['pɔndə] *v.* 默想，
　深思，考虑

⑤ vainly ['venli] *ad.* 白白
　地，枉然地

132

闲暇在动作时便是工作。
静止的海水荡动时便成波涛。

133

绿叶恋爱时便成了花。
花崇拜时便成了果实。

134

埋在地下的树根使树枝产生果实，却不要求什么
报酬。

135

阴雨的黄昏，风不休地吹着。
我看着摇曳的树枝，想念着万物的伟大。

136

子夜的风雨，如一个巨大的孩子，在不得时宜的黑
夜里醒来，开始游戏，和喊叫起来了。

137

海呀，你这暴风雨的孤寂的新妇呀，你虽掀起波浪
追随你的情人，但是无用呀。

138

"I am ashamed of my emptiness," said the Word to the Work.

"I know how poor I am when I see you," said the Work to the Word.

139

Time is the wealth of change, but the clock in its **parody**[1] makes it mere change and no wealth.

140

Truth in her dress finds facts too tight. In **fiction**[2] she moves with ease.

141

When I travelled to here and to there, I was tired of thee, O Road, but now when thou leadest me to everywhere I am wedded to thee in love.

142

Let me think that there is one among those stars that guides my life through the dark unknown.

138

文字对工作说道："我惭愧我的空虚。"

工作对文字说道："当我看见你时，我便知道我是怎样地贫乏了。"

139

时间是变化的财富，但时钟在它的游戏文章里却使它只不过是变化而没有财富。

① parody ['pærədi] *n.* 诙谐模仿的作品，拙劣的模仿

140

真理穿了衣裳觉得事实太拘束了，
在想象中，她却转动得很舒畅。

② fiction ['fikʃ(ə)n] *n.* 虚构

141

当我到这里，到那里地旅行着时，路呀，我厌倦了你了；但是现在，当你引导我到各处去时，我便爱上你，与你结婚了。

142

让我设想，在群星之中，有一颗星是指导着我的生命通过不可知的黑暗的。

143

Woman, with the **grace**[①] of your fingers you touched my things and order came out like music.

144

One sad voice has its nest among the **ruins**[②] of the years. It sings to me in the night, —"I loved you."

145

The **flaming**[③] fire warns me off by its own glow. Save me from the dying **embers**[④] hidden under ashes.

146

I have my stars in the sky, but oh for my little lamp unlit in my house.

147

The dust of the dead words clings to thee. Wash thy soul with silence.

148

Gaps are left in life through which comes the sad music of death.

① grace [greis] *n.* 优美，优雅

② ruin ['ru:in] *n.* 废墟，遗迹

③ flaming ['fleimiŋ] *a.* 燃烧的

④ ember ['embə] *n.* 余烬，余火

143

妇人，你用了你美丽的手指，触着我的器具，秩序便如音乐似的生出来了。

144

一个忧郁的声音，筑巢于逝水似的年华中。
它在夜里向我唱道，——"我爱你。"

145

燃着的火，以他的熊熊之光禁止我走近他。
把我从潜藏在灰中的余烬里救出来吧。

146

我有群星在天上，
但是，唉，我屋里的小灯却没有点亮。

147

死文字的尘土沾着你。
用沉默去洗净你的灵魂吧。

148

生命里留了许多罅隙，从这些罅隙中，送来了死之忧郁的音乐。

149

The world has opened its heart of light in the morning. Come out, my heart, with thy love to meet it.

150

My thoughts **shimmer**[1] with these shimmering leaves and my heart sings with the touch of this sunlight; my life is glad to be floating with all things into the blue of space, into the dark of time.

151

God's great power is in the gentle breeze, not in the storm.

152

This is a dream in which things are all loose and they **oppress**[2]. I shall find them gathered in thee when I awake and shall be free.

153

"Who is there to take up my duties?" asked the setting sun.
"I shall do what I can, my Master," said the earthen lamp.

154

By **plucking**[3] her **petals**[4] you do not gather the beauty of the flower.

149

世界已在早晨敞开了它的光明之心。
出来吧，我的心，带着你的爱去与它相会。

150

我的思想随着这些闪耀的绿叶而闪耀着，我的心灵
接触着这日光也唱了起来；我的生命因为偕了万物一同
浮泛在空间的蔚蓝，时间的墨黑中，正在快乐着呢。

① shimmer ['ʃimə] v. 发微
光，闪光

151

上帝的巨大的威权是在柔和的微飔里，而不在狂风
暴雨之中。

152

② oppress [ə'pres] v. 压迫，
使烦恼

在梦中，一切事都散漫着，都压着我，但这不过是
一个梦呀。当我醒来时，我便将觉得这些事都已聚集在
你那里，我也便将自由了。

153

落日问道："有谁在继续我的职务呢？"
瓦灯说道："我要尽我力之所能的做去，我的主人。"

③ pluck [plʌk] v. 采，摘，
拔

154

④ petal ['pet(ə)l] n. 花瓣

采着花瓣时，得不到花的美丽。

155

Silence will carry your voice like the nest that holds the sleeping birds.

156

The Great walks with the Small without fear.
The **Middling**① keeps **aloof**②.

157

The night opens the flowers in secret and allows the day to get thanks.

158

Power takes as **ingratitude**③ the **writhings**④ of its victims.

159

When we **rejoice**⑤ in our fullness, then we can part with our fruits with joy.

160

The raindrops kissed the earth and whispered, —"We are thy homesick children, mother, come back to thee from the heaven."

161

The **cobweb**⑥ pretends to catch dewdrops and catches flies.

155

沉默蕴蓄着语声，正如鸟巢拥围着睡鸟。

156

大的不怕与小的同游。
居中的却远而避之。

157

夜秘密地把花开放了，却让那白日去领受谢词。

158

权力认为牺牲者的痛苦是忘恩负义。

159

当我们以我们的充实为乐时，那么，我们便能很快乐地跟我们的果实分手了。

160

雨点与大地接吻，微语道，——"我们是你的思家的孩子，母亲，现在从天上回到你这里来了。"

161

蛛网好像要捉露点，却捉住了苍蝇。

① middling ['mid(ə)liŋ] *a.* 中等的

② aloof [ə'lu:f] *a.* 远离的，冷漠的

③ ingratitude [in'grætitju:d] *n.* 忘恩负义

④ writhing [raiðiŋ] *n.* 痛苦

⑤ rejoice [ri'dʒɔis] *v.* 欣喜，感到高兴

⑥ cobweb ['kɔbweb] *n.* 蜘蛛网，蜘蛛丝

162

Love! When you come with the burning lamp of pain in your hand, I can see your face and know you as **bliss**①.

163

"The **learned**② say that your lights will one day be no more," said the firefly to the stars. The stars made no answer.

164

In the **dusk**③ of the evening the bird of some early dawn comes to the nest of my silence.

165

Thoughts pass in my mind like **flocks**④ of lucks in the sky. I hear the voice of their wings.

166

The canal loves to think that rivers exist **solely**⑤ to supply it with water.

167

The world has kissed my soul with its pain, asking for its return in songs.

162

爱情呀！当你手里拿着点亮了的痛苦之灯走来时，我能够看见你的脸，而且以你为幸福。

163

萤火对天上的星道："学者说你的光明，总有一天会消灭的。"

天上的星不回答他。

164

在黄昏的微光里，有那清晨的鸟儿来到了我的沉默的鸟巢里。

165

思想掠过我的心上，如一群野鸭飞过天空。

我听见它们鼓翼之声了。

166

沟洫总喜欢想：河流的存在，是专为着供给它水流的。

167

世界以它的痛苦同我接吻，而要求歌声做报酬。

① bliss [blis] *n.* 洪福，极乐

② learned ['lə:nid] *a.* 有学问的，博学的

③ dusk [dʌsk] *n.* 黄昏，薄暮

④ flock [flɔk] *n.* 鸟群

⑤ solely ['səulli] *ad.* 仅仅，只

168

That which oppresses me, is it my soul trying to come out in the open, or the soul of the world knocking at my heart for its entrance?

169

Thought feeds itself with its own words and grows.

170

I have **dipped**[①] the vessel of my heart into this silent hour; it has filled with love.

171

Either you have work or you have not. When you have to say, "Let us do something", then begins mischief.

172

The sunflower **blushed**[②] to **own**[③] the nameless flower as her **kin**[④]. The sun rose and smiled on it, saying, "Are you well, my darling?"

173

"Who drives me forward like fate?"
"The Myself **striding**[⑤] on my back."

168

压迫着我的，到底是我的想要外出的灵魂呢，还是那世界的灵魂，敲着我心的门想要进来呢？

169

思想以它自己的言语喂养它自己，而成长起来。

170

我把我的心之碗轻轻浸入这沉默之时刻中，它充满了爱了。

171

或者你在做着工作，或者你没有。

当你不得不说："让我们做些事吧，"那么就要开始胡闹了。

172

向日葵羞于把无名的花朵看作她的同胞。

太阳升上来了，向它微笑，说道："你好么，我的宝贝儿？"

173

"谁如命运似的催着我向前走呢？"

"那是我自己，在身背后大跨步走着。"

① dip [dip] v. 将某物放入或伸入液体中

② blush [blʌʃ] v. 脸红，羞愧

③ own [əun] v. 承认

④ kin [kin] n. 家属，亲属，亲戚

⑤ stride [straid] v. 大步走，阔步行进

174

The clouds fill the water-cups of the river, hiding themselves in the distant hills.

175

I **spill**[①] water from my water-jar as I walk on my way. Very little remains for my home.

176

The water in a vessel is **sparkling**[②]; the water in the sea is dark. The small truth has words that are clear; the great truth has great silence.

177

Your smile was the flowers of your own fields, your talk was the rustle of your own mountain pines, but your heart was the woman that we all know.

178

It is the little things that I leave behind for my loved ones — great things are for everyone.

179

Woman, thou hast **encircled**[③] the world's heart with the depth of thy tears as the sea has the earth.

174

云把水倒在河的水杯里，它们自己却藏在远山之中。

175

我一路走去，从我的水瓶中漏出水来。
只留着极少极少的水供我家里用。

176

杯中的水是光辉的；海中的水却是黑色的。
小理可以用文字来说清楚，大理却只有沉默。

177

你的微笑是你自己田园里的花，你的谈吐是你自己山上的松林的萧萧，但是你的心呀，却是那个女人，那个我们全都认识的女人。

178

我把小小的礼物留给我所爱的人，——大的礼物却留给一切的人。

179

妇人呀，你用你的眼泪的深邃包绕着世界的心，正如大海包绕着大地。

① spill [spil] v. 泼洒，使溅出

② sparkle ['spɑːk(ə)l] v. 闪闪发光，闪耀

③ encircle [in'sɜːk(ə)l] v. 围绕，环绕

180

The sunshine **greets**[1] me with a smile. The rain, his sad sister, talks to my heart.

181

My flower of the day dropped its petals forgotten. In the evening it **ripens**[2] into a golden fruit of memory.

182

I am like the road in the night listening to the footfalls of its memories in silence.

183

The evening sky to me is like a window, and a lighted lamp, and a waiting behind it.

184

He who is too busy doing good finds no time to be good.

185

I am the autumn cloud, empty of rain, see my fullness in the field of ripened rice.

180

太阳以微笑向我问候。

雨，它的忧闷的妹妹，向我的心谈话。

181

我的昼间之花，落下它那被遗忘的花瓣。

在黄昏中，这花成熟为一颗记忆的金果。

182

我像那夜间之路，正静悄悄地听着记忆的足音。

183

　黄昏的天空，在我看来，像一扇窗户，一盏灯火，灯火背后的一次等待。

184

太急于做好事的人，反而找不到时间去做好事。

185

　我是秋云，空空的不载着雨水，但在成熟的稻田中，看见了我的充实。

① greet [gri:t] v. 向……致敬，问候，问好

② ripen ['raip(ə)n] v. 成熟

186

They hated and killed and men praised them. But God in shame **hastens**[1] to hide its memory under the green grass.

187

Toes are the fingers that have **forsaken**[2] their past.

188

Darkness travels towards light, but blindness towards death.

189

The pet dog **suspects**[3] the universe for **scheming**[4] to take its place.

190

Sit still, my heart, do not raise your dust. Let the world find its way to you.

191

The bow whispers to the arrow before it speeds **forth**[5]—"Your freedom is mine."

192

Woman, in your laughter you have the music of the fountain of life.

① hasten ['heis(ə)n] *v.* 赶快，赶紧，急忙

② forsaken [fə'seikən] *v.*（forsake 的过去分词）放弃，抛弃

③ suspect [sə'spekt] *v.* 怀疑，猜疑

④ scheme [ski:m] *v.* 策划，谋划

⑤ forth [fɔ:θ] *ad.* 向前，向前方

186

他们嫉妒，他们残杀，人反而称赞他们。

然而上帝却害了羞，匆匆地把他的记忆埋藏在绿草下面。

187

脚趾乃是舍弃了其过去的手指。

188

黑暗向光明旅行，但是盲者却向死亡旅行。

189

小狗疑心大宇宙阴谋篡夺它的位置。

190

静静地坐吧，我的心，不要扬起你的尘土。

让世界自己寻路向你走来。

191

弓在箭要射出之前，低声对箭说道，——"你的自由是我的。"

192

妇人，在你的笑声里有着生命之泉的音乐。

193

A mind all logic is like a knife all **blade**①. It makes the hand bleed that uses it.

194

God loves man's lamp-lights better than his own great stars.

195

This world is the world of wild storms kept **tame**② with the music of beauty.

196

"My heart is like the golden **casket**③ of thy kiss," said the sunset cloud to the sun.

197

By touching you may kill, by **keeping away**④ you may possess.

198

The **cricket's**⑤ **chirp**⑥ and the patter of rain come to me through the dark, like the rustle of dreams from my past youth.

193

全是理智的心，恰如一柄全是锋刃的刀。
叫使用它的人手上流血。

194

上帝爱人间的灯光甚于他自己的大星。

195

这世界乃是为美之音乐所驯服了的、狂风骤雨的
世界。

196

夕阳中的云彩向太阳说道："我的心经了你的接吻，
便似金的宝箱了。"

197

接触着，你许会杀害；远离着，你许会占有。

198

蟋蟀的唧唧，夜雨的淅沥，从黑暗中传到我的耳边，
好似我已逝的少年时代沙沙地来到我梦境中。

① blade [bleid] *n.* 刃，刀刃，刀锋

② tame [teim] *a.* 温顺的，柔顺的，顺从的

③ casket ['kɑ:skit] *n.* 小匣子，首饰盒

④ keep away 不靠近，远离

⑤ cricket ['krikit] *n.* 蟋蟀

⑥ chirp [tʃə:p] *n.*（鸟、虫等的）吱吱声，唧唧声

199

"I have lost my dewdrop," cries the flower to the morning sky that has lost all its stars.

200

The burning log **bursts**[1] in flame and cries, "This is my flower, my death."

201

The wasp thinks that the honey-**hive**[2] of the neighbouring bees is too small. His neighbours ask him to build one still smaller.

202

"I cannot keep your waves,"says the bank to the river.
"Let me keep your footprints in my heart."

203

The day, with the noise of this little earth, **drowns**[3] the silence of all worlds.

204

The song feels the **infinite**[4] in the air, the picture in the earth, the poem in the air and the earth;
For its words have meaning that walks and music that soars.

199

花朵向失落了它所有的星辰的曙天叫道："我的露点全失落了。"

200

燃烧着的木块，熊熊地生出火光，叫道，——"这是我的花朵，我的死亡。"

201

黄蜂以邻蜂储蜜之巢为太小。
它的邻人要它去建筑一个更小的。

202

河岸向河流说道："我不能留住你的波浪。"
"让我保存你的足印在我心里吧。"

203

白日以这小小地球的喧扰，淹没了整个宇宙的沉默。

204

歌声在空中感得无限，图画在地上感得无限，诗呢，无论在空中，在地上都是如此；
因为诗的词句含有能走动的意义与能飞翔的音乐。

① burst [bə:st] *v.* 爆发，迸发，突然发生

② hive [haiv] *n.* 蜂巢，蜂房

③ drown [draun] *v.* （声音等）盖过，盖没，压过

④ infinite ['infinət] *a.* 无限的，无穷的

205

When the sun goes down to the West, the East of his morning stands before him in silence.

206

Let me not put myself wrongly to my world and **set** it **against**[1] me.

207

Praise shames me, for I secretly beg for it.

208

Let my doing nothing when I have nothing to do become **untroubled**[2] in its depth of peace like the evening in the seashore when the water is silent.

209

Maiden[3], your **simplicity**[4], like the blueness of the lake, **reveals**[5] your depth of truth.

210

The best does not come alone. It comes with the **company**[6] of the all.

205

太阳在西方落下时，它的早晨的东方已静悄悄地站在它面前。

206

让我不要错误地把自己放在我的世界里而使它反对我。

207

荣誉羞着我，因为我暗地里求着它。

208

当我没有什么事做时，便让我不做什么事，不受骚扰地沉入安静深处吧，一如那海水沉默时海边的暮色。

209

少女呀，你的纯朴，如湖水之碧，表现出你的真理之深邃。

210

最好的东西不是独来的。
他伴了所有的东西同来。

① set ... against ... 使……反对或敌视……

② untroubled [ʌn'trʌb(ə)ld] *a.* 无烦恼的，未被扰乱的，平静的

③ maiden ['meid(ə)n] *n.* 少女，年轻姑娘

④ simplicity [sim'plisiti] *n.* 朴素，质朴

⑤ reveal [ri'vi:l] *v.* 揭示，展现

⑥ company ['kʌmp(ə)ni] *n.* 陪伴

211

God's right hand is gentle, but **terrible**[1] is his left hand.

212

My evening came among the alien trees and spoke in a language which my morning stars did not know.

213

Night's darkness is a bag that **bursts**[2] with the gold of the dawn.

214

Our desire lends the colours of the rainbow to the mere mists and **vapours**[3] of life.

215

God waits to win back his own flowers as gifts from man's hands.

216

My sad thoughts **tease**[4] me asking me their own names.

211

上帝的右手是慈爱的，但是他的左手却可怕。

212

我的晚色从陌生的树木中走来，它用我的晓星所不懂得的语言说话。

213

夜之黑暗是一只口袋，盛满了发出黎明的金光的口袋。

214

我们的欲望，把彩虹的颜色，借给那只不过是云雾的人生。

215

上帝等待着要从人的手上把他自己的花朵作为礼物赢得回去。

216

我的忧思缠扰着我，要问我它们自己的名字。

① terrible ['terib(ə)l] *a.* 可怕的，骇人的

② burst [bə:st] *v.* 爆裂，胀裂，胀破

③ vapour ['veipə] *n.* 蒸气，汽

④ tease [ti:z] *v.* 强求

217

The service of the fruit is precious, the service of the flower is sweet, but let my service be the service of the leaves in its shade of humble **devotion**[①].

218

My heart has spread its sails to the idle winds for the shadowy island of Anywhere.

219

Men are **cruel**[②], but Man is kind.

220

Make me thy cup and let my fullness be for thee and for thine.

221

The storm is like the cry of some god in pain whose love the earth refuses.

222

The world does not **leak**[③] because death is not a **crack**[④].

217

果实的事业是尊贵的，花的事业是甜美的，但是让我做叶的事业罢，叶是谦逊地专心地垂着绿荫的。

218

我的心向着阑珊的风，张了帆，要到无论何处的荫凉之岛去。

219

独夫们是凶暴的，但人民是善良的。

220

把我当作你的杯吧，让我为了你，而且为了你的人而盛满了水吧。

221

狂风暴雨像是那因他的爱情被大地所拒绝而在痛苦中的天神的哭声。

222

世界不会裂开，因为死亡并不是一个罅隙。

① devotion [di'vəuʃ(ə)n] n. 献身，奉献

② cruel [kruəl] a. 残酷的，残忍的，残暴的

③ leak [li:k] v.（容器）漏

④ crack [kræk] n. 裂缝，裂纹

223

Life has become richer by the love that has been lost.

224

My friend, your great heart shone with the sunrise of the East like the snowy **summit**[①] of a lonely hill in the dawn.

225

The fountain of death makes the still water of life play.

226

Those who have everything but thee, my God, laugh at those who have nothing but thyself.

227

The movement of life has its rest in its own music.

228

Kicks only raise dust and not crops from the earth.

223

生命因为失去了爱情，而更为富足。

224

我的朋友，你伟大的心闪射出东方朝阳的光芒，正如黎明中一个积雪的孤峰。

225

死之流泉，使生的止水跳跃。

226

那些有一切东西而没有您的人，我的上帝，在讥笑着那些没有别的东西而只有您的人呢。

227

生命的运动在它自己的音乐里得到它的休息。

228

踢足只能从地上扬起灰尘而不能得到收获。

① summit ['sʌmit] *n.* 最高峰，极顶，最高点

229

Our names are the light that **glows**[1] on the sea waves at night and then dies without leaving its signature.

230

Let him only see the **thorns**[2] who has eyes to see the rose.

231

Set the bird's wings **with**[3] gold and it will never again soar in the sky.

232

The same lotus of our **clime**[4] blooms here in the alien water with the same sweetness, under another name.

233

In heart's **perspective**[5] the distance **looms**[6] large.

234

The moon has her light all over the sky, her dark spots to herself.

235

Do not say, "It is morning," and **dismiss**[7] it with a name of yesterday. See it for the first time as a newborn child that has no name.

229

我们的名字，便是夜里海波上发出的光，痕迹也不留地就泯灭了。

230

让睁眼看着玫瑰花的人也看看它的刺。

231

鸟翼上系上了黄金，这鸟便永不能再在天上翱翔了。

232

我们地方的荷花又在这里陌生的水上开了花，放出同样的清香，只是名字换了。

233

在心的远景里，那相隔的距离显得更广阔了。

234

月儿把她的光明遍照在天上，却留着她的黑斑给她自己。

235

不要说"这是早晨了"，就用一个"昨天"的名词把它打发掉。把它当作第一次看到的还没有名字的新生孩子吧。

① glow [gləu] v. 发光，放光，发热

② thorn [θɔ:n] n. 刺，棘

③ set ... with ... 将……镶嵌到……上

④ clime [klaim] n. 地带，地区

⑤ perspective [pə'spektiv] n. 远景，景

⑥ loom [lu:m] v. 隐约可见

⑦ dismiss [dis'mis] v. 把……打发走，不予理会

236

Smoke boasts to the sky, and ashes to the earth, that they are brothers to the fire.

237

The raindrop whispered to the **jasmine**[①], "Keep me in your heart for ever." The jasmine sighed, "Alas," and dropped to the ground.

238

Timid[②] thoughts, do not be afraid of me. I am a poet.

239

The **dim**[③] silence of my mind seems filled with crickets' chirp—the grey **twilight**[④] of sound.

240

Rockets, your insult to the stars follows yourself back to the earth.

241

Thou hast led me through my crowded travels of the day to my evening's loneliness. I wait for its meaning through the stillness of the night.

236

青烟对天空夸口，灰烬对大地夸口，都以为它们是火的兄弟。

237

雨点向茉莉花微语道："把我永久地留在你的心里吧。"

茉莉花叹息了一声，落在地上了。

238

恧怯的思想呀，不要怕我。

我是一个诗人。

239

我的心在朦胧的沉默里，似乎充满了蟋蟀的鸣声——那灰色的微明的歌声。

240

爆竹呀，你对于群星的侮蔑，又跟了你自己回到地上来了。

241

您曾经带领着我，穿过我的白天的拥挤不堪的旅行，而到达了我的黄昏的孤寂之境。

在通宵的寂静里，我等待着它的意义。

① jasmine ['dʒæzmin] *n.* 茉莉

② timid ['timid] *a.* 胆怯的，腼腆的

③ dim [dim] *a.* 模糊不清的

④ twilight ['twailait] *n.* 薄暮，暮色

242

This life is the crossing of a sea, where we meet in the same narrow ship. In death we reach the shore and go to our different worlds.

243

The stream of truth flows through its channels of mistakes.

244

My heart is homesick today for the one sweet hour across the sea of time.

245

The bird-song is the echo of the morning light back from the earth.

246

"Are you too proud to kiss me?" the morning light asks the **buttercup**[1].

247

"How may I sing to thee and worship, O Sun?" asked the little flower. "By the simple silence of thy **purity**[2]," answered the sun.

242

我们的生命就似渡过一个大海，我们都相聚在这个狭小的舟中。

死时，我们便到了岸，各往各的世界去了。

243

真理之川从他的错误之沟渠中流过。

244

今天我的心是在想家了，在想着那跨过时间之海的那一个甜蜜的时候。

245

鸟的歌声是曙光从大地反响过去的回声。

246

晨光问毛茛道："你是不是骄傲得不肯和我接吻么？"

247

小花问道："我要怎样地对你唱，怎样地崇拜你呢？太阳呀？"

太阳答道："只要用你的纯洁的简朴的沉默。"

① buttercup ['bʌtəkʌp] *n.* 毛茛属植物

② purity ['pjuəriti] *n.* 洁净，纯洁

248

Man is worse than an animal when he is an animal.

249

Dark clouds become heaven's flowers when kissed by light.

250

Let not the sword-blade mock its handle for being **blunt**[①].

251

The night's silence, like a deep lamp, is burning with the light of its **milky way**[②].

252

Around the sunny island of life **swells**[③] day and night death's limitless song of the sea.

253

Is not this mountain like a flower, with its petals of hills, drinking the sunlight?

254

The real with its meaning read wrong and **emphasis**[④] **misplaced**[⑤] is the unreal.

248

当人是兽时，他比兽还坏。

249

黑云受光的接吻时便变成天上的花朵。

250

不要让刀锋讥笑它柄子的拙钝。

251

夜的沉默，如一个深深的灯盏，银河便是它燃着的灯光。

252

死像大海的无限的歌声，日夜冲击着生命的光明岛的四周。

253

花瓣似的山峰在饮着日光，这山岂不像一朵花吗？

254

"真实"的含义被误解、轻重被倒置，那就成了"不真实"。

① blunt [blʌnt] *a.* 钝的，不锋利的

② milky way 银河

③ swell [swel] *v.* （海水）高涨，波涛汹涌

④ emphasis ['emfəsis] *n.* 重点

⑤ misplace [mis'pleis] *v.* 把……放错地方

255

Find your beauty, my heart, from the world's movement, like the boat that has the grace of the wind and the water.

256

The eyes are not proud of their sight but of their eyeglasses.

257

I live in this little world of mine and am afraid to make it the least less. Lift me into thy world and let me have the freedom gladly to lose my all.

258

The false can never grow into truth by growing in power.

259

My heart, with its **lapping**[①] waves of song, longs to **caress**[②] this green world of the sunny day.

260

Wayside grass, love the star, then your dreams will come out in flowers.

255

我的心呀，从世界的流动中，找你的美吧，正如那小船得到风与水的优美似的。

256

眼不以能视来骄人，却以它们的眼镜来骄人。

257

我住在我的这个小小的世界里，生怕使它再缩小一丁点儿了。把我抬举到您的世界里去吧，让我有高高兴兴地失去我的一切的自由。

258

虚伪永远不能凭借它生长在权力中而变成真实。

259

我的心，同着它的歌的拍拍舐岸的波浪，渴望着要抚爱这个阳光熙和的绿色世界。

260

道旁的草，爱那天上的星吧，那么，你的梦境便可在花朵里实现了。

① lap ['læp] v.（波浪）拍打

② caress [kə'res] v. 爱抚，抚摸

261

Let your music, like a sword, **pierce**① the noise of the market to its heart.

262

The **trembling**② leaves of this tree touch my heart like the fingers of an infant child.

263

The little flower lies in the dust. It **sought**③ the path of the butterfly.

264

I am in the world of the roads. The night comes. Open thy gate, thou world of the home.

265

I have sung the songs of thy day. In the evening let me carry thy lamp through the stormy path.

266

I do not ask thee into the house. Come into my infinite loneliness, my Lover.

261

让你的音乐如一柄利刃，直刺入市井喧扰的心中吧。

262

这树的颤动之叶，触动着我的心，像一个婴儿的
手指。

263

小花睡在尘土里。
它寻求蛱蝶走的道路。

264

我是在道路纵横的世界上。
夜来了。打开您的门吧，家之世界啊。

265

我已经唱过了您的白天的歌。
在黄昏时候，让我拿着您的灯走过风雨飘摇的道
路吧。

266

我不要求你进我的屋里。
你且到我无量的孤寂里吧，我的爱人！

① pierce [piəs] v. 刺穿，刺破

② tremble ['tremb(ə)l] v. 发抖，打战

③ sought [sɔːt] v.（seek 的过去式和过去分词）寻求，寻找

267

Death belongs to life as birth does. The walk is in the raising of the foot as in the laying of it down.

268

I have learnt the simple meaning of thy whispers in flowers and sunshine — teach me to know thy words in pain and death.

269

The night's flower was late when the morning kissed her, she **shivered**[1] and sighed and dropped to the ground.

270

Through the sadness of all things I hear the **crooning**[2] of the Eternal Mother.

271

I came to your shore as a stranger, I lived in your house as a guest, I leave your door as a friend, my earth.

272

Let my thoughts come to you, when I am gone, like the **afterglow**[3] of sunset at the **margin**[4] of **starry**[5] silence.

267

死之隶属于生命，正与出生一样。

举足是在走路，正如放下足也是在走路。

268

我已经学会了你在花与阳光里微语的意义。——再教我明白你在苦与死中所说的话吧。

269

夜的花朵来晚了，当早晨吻着她时，她战栗着，叹息了一声，萎落在地上了。

270

从万物的愁苦中，我听见了"永恒母亲"的呻吟。

271

大地呀，我到你岸上时是一个陌生人，住在你屋内的是一个宾客，离开你的门时是一个朋友。

272

当我去时，让我的思想到你那里来，如那夕阳的余光，映在沉默的星天的边上。

① shiver ['ʃivə] v. 颤抖，打战

② croon [kru:n] v. 低声哼唱，呻吟

③ afterglow ['ɑ:ftəgləu] n. 余晖，夕照

④ margin ['mɑ:dʒin] n. 边缘

⑤ starry ['stɑ:ri] a. 多星的，布满星星的

273

Light in my heart the evening star of rest and then let the night whisper to me of love.

274

I am a child in the dark. I **stretch**[1] my hands through the **coverlet**[2] of night for thee, Mother.

275

The day of work is done. Hide my face in your arms, Mother.
Let me dream.

276

The lamp of meeting burns long; it **goes out**[3] in a moment at the parting.

277

One word keep for me in thy silence, O World, when I am dead, "I have loved."

278

We live in this world when we love it.

273

在我的心头燃点起那休憩的黄昏星吧，然后让黑夜向我微语着爱情。

274

我是一个在黑暗中的孩子。

我从夜的被单里向您伸出我的双手，母亲。

275

白天的工作完了。把我的脸掩藏在您的臂间吧，母亲。让我做梦。

276

集会时的灯光，点了很久，会散时，灯便立刻灭了。

277

当我死时，世界呀，请在你的沉默中，替我留着"我已经爱过了"这句话吧。

278

我们在热爱世界时便生活在这世界上。

① stretch [stretʃ] *v.* 伸出

② coverlet ['kʌvəlit] *n.* 床罩，被单

③ go out 熄灭

279

Let the dead have the **immortality**[1] of fame, but the living the immortality of love.

280

I have seen thee as the half-awakened child sees his mother in the dusk of the dawn and then smiles and sleeps again.

281

I shall die again and again to know that life is **inexhaustible**[2].

282

While I was passing with the crowd in the road I saw thy smile from the **balcony**[3] and I sang and forgot all noise.

283

Love is life in its fullness like the cup with its wine.

284

They light their own lamps and sing their own words in their temples. But the birds sing thy name in thine own morning light —for thy name is joy.

279

让死者有那不朽的名，但让生者有那不朽的爱。

280

我看见你，像那半醒的婴孩在黎明的微光里看见他的母亲，于是微笑而又睡去了。

281

我将死了又死，以明白生是无穷无竭的。

282

当我和拥挤的人群一同在路上走过时，我看见您从洋台[1]上送过来的微笑，我歌唱着，忘却了所有的喧哗。

283

爱就是充实了的生命，正如盛满了酒的酒杯。

284

他们点了他们自己的灯，在他们的寺院内，吟唱他们自己的话语。

但是小鸟们却在你的晨光中，唱着你的名字，——因为你的名字便是快乐。

1　现写作"阳台"。

① immortality [imɔ:'tæliti] *n.* 不朽，不死，永存

② inexhaustible [inig'zɔ:stib(ə)l] *a.* 无穷尽的

③ balcony ['bælkəni] *n.* 阳台

285

Lead me in the centre of thy silence to fill my heart with songs.

286

Let them live who choose in their own **hissing**[1] world of fireworks. My heart longs for thy stars, my God.

287

Love's pain sang round my life like the **unplumbed**[2] sea, and love's joy sang like birds in its flowering **groves**[3].

288

Put out the lamp when thou wishest. I shall know thy darkness and shall love it.

289

When I stand before thee at the day's end thou shalt see my scars and know that I had my wounds and also my healing.

290

Some day I shall sing to thee in the sunrise of some other world, "I have seen thee before in the light of the earth, in the love of man."

285

领我到您的沉寂的中心，使我的心充满了歌吧。

286

让那些选择了他们自己的焰火咝咝的世界的，就生活在那里吧。

我的心渴望着您的繁星，我的上帝。

287

爱的痛苦环绕着我的一生，像汹涌的大海似的唱着，而爱的快乐却像鸟儿们在花林里似的唱着。

288

假如您愿意，您就熄了灯吧。

我将明白您的黑暗，而且将喜爱它。

289

当我在那日子的终了，站在您的面前时，您将看见我的伤疤，而知道我有我的许多创伤，但也有我的医治的法儿。

290

总有一天，我要在别的世界的晨光里对你唱道："我以前在地球的光里，在人的爱里，已经见过你了。"

① hissing ['hisiŋ] *a.* 发嘶嘶声的

② unplumbed [ʌn'plʌmd] *a.* 未经探测的

③ grove [grəuv] *n.* 小树林，树丛

291

Clouds come floating into my life from other days no longer to **shed**[1] rain or **usher**[2] storm but to give colour to my sunset sky.

292

Truth raises against itself the storm that **scatters**[3] its seeds **broadcast**[4].

293

The storm of the last night has **crowned**[5] this morning with golden peace.

294

Truth seems to come with its final word; and the final word gives birth to its next.

295

Blessed is he whose fame does not **outshine**[6] his truth.

296

Sweetness of thy name fills my heart when I forget mine—like thy morning sun when the mist is melted.

291

从别的日子里飘浮到我的生命里的黑云，不再落下雨点或引起风暴了，却只给予我的夕阳的天空以色彩。

292

真理引起了反对它自己的狂风骤雨，那场风雨吹散了真理的广播的种子。

293

昨夜的风雨给今日的早晨戴上了金色的和平。

294

真理仿佛带了它的结论而来；而那结论却产生了它的第二个。

295

他是有福的，因为他的名望并没有比他的真实更光亮。

296

您的名字的甜蜜充溢着我的心，而我忘掉了我自己的——就像您的早晨的太阳升起时，那大雾便消失了。

① shed [ʃed] v. 使流出，使涌出

② usher ['ʌʃə] v. 引导，带领

③ scatter ['skætə] v. 散布，撒播

④ broadcast ['brɔ:dkɑ:st] ad. 四散地

⑤ crown [kraun] v. 给……加顶，装在……顶上

⑥ outshine [aut'ʃain] v. 比……更亮，比……更灿烂

297

The silent night has the beauty of the mother and the **clamorous**[①] day of the child.

298

The world loved man when he smiled. The world became afraid of him when he laughed.

299

God waits for man to **regain**[②] his childhood in wisdom.

300

Let me feel this world as thy love **taking form**[③], then my love will help it.

301

Thy sunshine smiles upon the winter days of my heart, never doubting of its spring flowers.

302

God kisses the **finite**[④] in his love and man the infinite.

297

静悄悄的黑夜具有母亲的美丽，而吵闹的白天具有孩子的美。

298

当人微笑时，世界爱了他。但他大笑时，世界便怕他了。

299

上帝等待着人在智慧中重新获得童年。

300

让我感到这个世界乃是您的爱的成形吧，那么，我的爱也将帮助着它。

301

您的太阳光对着我的心头的冬天微笑着，从来不怀疑它的春天的花朵。

302

上帝在他的爱里吻着"有涯"，而人却吻着"无涯"。

① clamorous ['klæmərəs] *a.* 吵闹的，叫喊的，嘈杂的

② regain [ri'gein] *v.* 收回，领回，重新获得

③ take form 成形

④ finite ['fainait] *a.* 有限的

303

Thou crossest desert lands of **barren**[1] years to reach the moment of **fulfillment**[2].

304

God's silence ripens man's thoughts into speech.

305

Thou wilt find, Eternal Traveller, marks of thy footsteps across my songs.

306

Let me not shame thee, Father, who displayest thy glory in thy children.

307

Cheerless[3] is the day, the light under frowning clouds is like a punished child with traces of tears on its pale cheeks, and the cry of the wind is like the cry of a wounded world. But I know I am travelling to meet my Friend.

308

Tonight there is a stir among the palm leaves, a **swell**[4] in the sea, Full Moon, like the heart-**throb**[5] of the world. From what unknown sky hast thou carried in thy silence the aching secret of love?

303

您横越过不毛之年的沙漠而到达了圆满的时刻。

304

上帝的静默使人的思想成熟而为语言。

305

"永恒的旅客"呀，你可以在我的歌中找到你的足迹。

306

让我不至羞辱您吧，父亲，您在您的孩子们身上显现出您的光荣。

307

这一天是不快活的，光在蹙额的云下，如一个被打的儿童，在灰白的脸上留着泪痕，风又号叫着似一个受伤的世界的哭声。但是我知道我正跋涉着去会我的朋友。

308

今天晚上棕榈叶在嚓嚓地作响，海上有大浪，满月呵，就像世界在心脉悸跳。从什么不可知的天空，您在您的沉默里带来了爱的痛苦的秘密？

① barren ['bær(ə)n] *a.* 贫瘠的，不毛的，荒芜的

② fulfillment [ful'filmənt] *n.* 实现，完成

③ cheerless ['tʃiəlis] *a.* 阴郁的，惨淡的

④ swell [swel] *n.* 海涌，浪涌

⑤ throb [θrɔb] *n.*（心脏等急速地）跳动，悸动，搏动

309

I dream of a star, an island of light, where I shall be born and in the depth of its **quickening**[1] leisure my life will ripen its works like the rice-field in the autumn sun.

310

The smell of the wet earth in the rain rises like a great **chant**[2] of praise from the voiceless **multitude**[3] of the **insignificant**[4].

311

That love can ever lose is a fact that we cannot accept as truth.

312

We shall know some day that death can never rob us of that which our soul has gained, for her **gains**[5] are one with herself.

313

God comes to me in the dusk of my evening with the flowers from my past kept fresh in his basket.

314

When all the strings of my life will be **tuned**[6], my Master, then at every touch of thine will come out the music of love.

309

我梦见了一颗星，一个光明的岛屿，我将在那里出生，而在它的快速的闲暇的深处，我的生命将成熟它的事业，像在秋天的阳光之下的稻田。

310

雨中的湿土的气息，就像从渺小的无声的群众那里来的一阵子巨大的赞美歌声。

311

说爱情会失去的那句话，乃是我们不能够当作真理来接受的一个事实。

312

我们将有一天会明白，死永远不能够夺去我们的灵魂所获得的东西，因为她所获得的，和她自己是一体。

313

上帝在我的黄昏的微光中，带着花到我这里来，这些花都是我过去之时的，在他的花篮中，还保存得很新鲜。

314

主呀，当我的生之琴弦都已调得谐和时，你的手的一弹一奏，都可以发出爱的乐声来。

① quickening ['kwikəniŋ] a. 加速的，使活泼的

② chant [tʃɑ:nt] n. 歌曲，旋律

③ multitude ['mʌltitju:d] n. 许多，大量

④ insignificant [insig'nifik(ə)nt] a. 不重要的，无足轻重的

⑤ gain [gein] n. 获得物

⑥ tune [tju:n] v. 校准（乐器的）音调，为（乐器）调音

315

Let me live truly, my Lord, so that death to me becomes true.

316

Man's history is waiting in patience for the **triumph**[1] of the insulted man.

317

I feel thy gaze upon my heart this moment like the sunny silence of the morning upon the lonely field whose harvest is over.

318

I long for the Island of Songs across this **heaving**[2] Sea of Shouts.

319

The **prelude**[3] of the night is **commenced**[4] in the music of the sunset, in its **solemn**[5] **hymn**[6] to the **ineffable**[7] dark.

320

I have **scaled**[8] the peak and found no shelter in fame's **bleak**[9] and barren height. Lead me, my Guide, before the light fades, into the valley of quiet where life's harvest **mellows**[10] into golden wisdom.

315

让我真真实实地活着吧，我的上帝，这样，死对于我也就成了真实的了。

316

人类的历史在很忍耐地等待着被侮辱者的胜利。

317

我这一刻感到你的眼光正落在我的心上，像那早晨阳光中的沉默落在已收获的孤寂的田野上一样。

318

我渴望着歌的岛屿立在这喧哗的波涛起伏的海中。

319

夜的序曲是开始于夕阳西下的音乐，开始于它的向难以形容的黑暗的庄严的赞歌。

320

我攀登上高峰，发现在名誉的荒芜不毛的高处，简直找不到遮身之地。我的导引者啊，领导着我在光明逝去之前，进到沉静的山谷里去吧，在那里，生的收获成熟为黄金的智慧。

① triumph ['traiʌmf] *n.* 凯旋，胜利

② heaving ['hi:viŋ] *a.* 起伏的

③ prelude ['prelju:d] *n.* 序曲，前奏曲

④ commence [kə'mens] *v.* 开始

⑤ solemn ['sɔləm] *a.* 严肃的，庄重的

⑥ hymn [him] *n.* 赞歌，颂歌

⑦ ineffable [in'efəb(ə)l] *a.* 言语难以表达、难以形容的

⑧ scale [skeil] *v.* 攀登

⑨ bleak [bli:k] *a.* 荒凉的

⑩ mellow ['meləu] *v.* 变得成熟

321

Things look **phantastic**[1] in this dimness of the dusk—the **spires**[2] whose bases are lost in the dark and tree-tops like **blots**[3] of ink. I shall wait for the morning and wake up to see thy city in the light.

322

I have suffered and **despaired**[4] and known death and I am glad that I am in this great world.

323

There are **tracts**[5] in my life that are **bare**[6] and silent. They are the open spaces where my busy days had their light and air.

324

Release[7] me from my unfulfilled past clinging to me from behind making death difficult.

325

Let this be my last word, that I trust in thy love.

① phantastic [fæn'tæstik] *a.* 梦幻的

② spire [spaiə] *n.* 尖塔

③ blot [blɔt] *n.* 污渍

④ despair [di'spɛə] *v.* 绝望

⑤ tract [trækt] *n.* 地带，地域

⑥ bare [bɛə] *a.* 光秃的

⑦ release [ri'li:s] *v.* 释放；解放

321

在这个黄昏的朦胧里，好些东西看来都有些幻相——尖塔的底层在黑暗里消失了，树顶像墨水的斑点似的。我将等待着黎明，而当我醒来的时候，就会看到在光明里的您的城市。

322

我曾经受苦过，曾经失望过，曾经体会过"死亡"，于是我以我在这伟大的世界里为乐。

323

在我的一生里，也有贫乏和沉默的地域。它们是我忙碌的日子得到日光与空气的几片空旷之地。

324

我的未完成的过去，从后边缠绕到我身上，使我难于死去，请从它那里释放了我吧。

325

"我相信你的爱。"让这句话做我的最后的话。